Hare Jo
Home Guard

Alison Uttley
pictures by Margaret Tempest

FOREWORD

Of course you must understand that Grey Rabbit's home had no electric light or gas, and even the candles were made from pith of rushes dipped in wax from the wild bees' nests, which Squirrel found. Water there was in plenty, but it did not come from a tap. It flowed from a spring outside, which rose up from the ground and went to a brook. Grey Rabbit cooked on a fire, but it was a wood fire, there was no coal in that part of the country. Tea did not come from India, but from a little herb known very well to country people, who once dried it and used it in their cottage homes. Bread was baked from corn ears, ground fine, and Hare and Grey Rabbit gleaned in the cornfields to get the wheat.

The doormats were plaited rushes, like country-made mats, and cushions were stuffed with wool gathered from the hedges where sheep pushed through the thorns. As for the looking-glass, Grey Rabbit found the glass, dropped from a lady's handbag, and Mole made a frame for it. Usually the animals gazed at themselves in the still pools as so many country children have done. The country ways of Grey Rabbit were the country ways known to the author.

Squirrel and Hare sat at the table waiting for breakfast. The toast was made, and the kettle was boiling on the fire. Little Grey Rabbit warmed the tea-pot and put in three spoonfuls of daisy tea. She poured the boiling water over it and placed it on the table under the tea-cosy. Then she gave Hare a big bunch of lettuce, and Squirrel a middle-sized bunch, and on her own plate she put brown bread, honey and nuts, and a pat of yellow butter from the Alderney cow.

"Where's the milk, Grey Rabbit?" asked Hare. "We can't drink tea without milk."

He munched lettuce noisily and frowned.

"Where's Old Hedgehog?" asked Squirrel, delicately cracking a nut.

"I'll see if he's coming," said Grey Rabbit. "He has never been as late as this. Something must have happened. I hope Fuzzypeg is all right."

"Oh Fuzzypeg was rolling down the field like a fat little barrel last night," said Hare. "There's nothing the matter with that young fellow."

Grey Rabbit ran to the door and looked about her. Then she spied Hedgehog the milkman. He was trotting quickly along the lane with his cans of milk. His spotted scarf fluttered in the wind and his white smock billowed behind him like a sail.

"Good morning, Hedgehog," called Grey Rabbit, and she went to meet him.

"Good morning, miss," panted Hedgehog. "I'm late as never was. Have you heard the news? Oh my!"

He stamped up the path and looked through the doorway at Squirrel and Hare. He put down the milk cans and waited for Grey Rabbit to get her jug.

"Have you heard the news?" he asked importantly.

"What news?" asked Hare, and he held up his empty mug. "We want milk, not news."

"There nearly was no milk. Nearly was never a drop," replied Hedgehog crossly. He filled Grey Rabbit's jug and then stood gazing very sternly at all of them.

"What's the matter, dear Hedgehog?" asked Grey Rabbit anxiously.

"There's a war," said Hedgehog. "That's what's the matter. A war!"

"A war? What's that?" asked Hare, puzzled.

"A war's a battle coming on us. Yes! Cows was that upset they kicked over my bucket when I told 'em and toppled me over, and I had to begin milking all over again."

"Why were the cows upset?" asked Grey Rabbit.

"Because there's a war! Bang! Bang! Cows don't like a noise."

"Who is going to make a noise?" asked Grey Rabbit.

"Nay, I don't know. Somebody's on the warpath. I'm off to find out. Keep indoors and mind yourselves. Good day to you all."

Squirrel, Hare and little Grey Rabbit all ate their crisp lettuce and toast.

"Perhaps it's a Fox or a Weasel on the warpath" said Hare.

"Perhaps it's a Wolf," faltered Squirrel.

"Or a mad bull," went on Hare.

Tap! Rat-a-tap-tap! There was a flutter of wings and Robin the Postman appeared on the doorstep. He held out a leafy letter to Grey Rabbit. "Have you heard the news?" he asked. He whistled a merry marching song and kept time with his foot.

"Yes. There's a war!" cried the three friends all together. "Tell us about it, Robin."

"It's a war of Weasels. There's an army of them coming to attack us. They are coming through the far-away woods to invade our peaceful little land."

He shook his post-bag and showed them all the leaves which brimmed it.

"All these letters to deliver this morning," he boasted. "Everybody's got a letter today. We've all got to wake up and arm ourselves with spears and arrows against the invading Weasels."

Away he flew, and out of his bag frisked the letters, dropping into holes in the bank, fluttering through green doorways and open windows, telling the animal world that the Weasels were coming and that they must fight them.

"Dear! Dear!" cried Squirrel. "I shall fight with these." She picked up her knitting needles and began to knit a stocking at a great rate.

"Pooh!" scoffed Hare. "I shall use my catapult. Then I needn't go too close to their sharp teeth."

Grey Rabbit was staring at the little crooked words traced on the leaf.

"Let me look," said Squirrel and peered at the writing.

"I wish I were a scholar like you, Grey Rabbit. I can't read those long words. What does it say?"

"Courage! Fight for freedom." Grey Rabbit read the letter slowly.

"Courage!" echoed Hare. "I'll learn those Weasels!"

He picked up the poker and flourished it in the air.

They were making the beds when there was a pitter-patter of little feet at the door.

"Goodness me! The enemy is here!" shrieked Hare, and he and Squirrel dived under their beds, leaving Grey Rabbit to face the army.

She peeped through the keyhole, and there stood her old friends, Moldy Warp and Water-rat, with a company of rabbits and squirrels from the woods.

"We've come to hold a council of war," said Moldy Warp, and he rapped on the door.

"Who goes there?" called Squirrel in a faint squeak.

"Friend or foe?" called Hare in a thin high voice.

"It's Moldy Warp," laughed Grey Rabbit and she flung wide the door.

There wasn't room inside for so many, so they sat in the garden.

"The Weasels are on the warpath," said Moldy Warp.

"Where is the warpath?" asked the rabbits.

"It's that long lane, the old Roman road, which runs through the woods to the hills, as straight as an arrow. It comes close to your house, Grey Rabbit."

Mrs Hedgehog and her husband came hurrying up, and the Speckledy Hen bustled through the gate with a loud cluck. She was helping Fuzzypeg to carry a basket of eggs.

"We've brought ammunition," said Fuzzypeg, panting up the path. "We've brought these to throw at the Weasels."

"These are old-laid eggs," explained the Speckledy Hen. "The Hen-that-always-lays-astray left them long ago in the hedge."

"Capital!" cried the Mole. "They will be deadly! Bring more if you can, Speckledy Hen."

The Hen clucked proudly and said that she knew of quite a number of ancient brown eggs hidden in corners of wood-piles and haystacks.

"Now for our own little army." The Mole looked round at the company of excited, quivering little animals.

"Hare! You shall be the Home Guard! You must defend Grey Rabbit's house and all our homes with your life."

Hare shivered, but he drew himself up proudly.

"Squirrel," said Mole, "you must knit socks and stockings and mittens and scarves for all our fighters."

Squirrel nodded and clicked her needles.

"Grey Rabbit! You must be a nurse, and take care of the wounded."

Grey Rabbit turned up her sleeves and all the little rabbits were glad that Grey Rabbit would take care of them.

"What about me?" asked Hedgehog. "I may be old, but I can fight."

"You are a brave fellow, Hedgehog," nodded Mole. "I shall want you to be a leader, a captain. Water-rat will guard the river banks. Wise Owl will fly over the woods and watch for the approach of the enemy. All the rest of the animals will be fighters, hidden on the warpath with bows and arrows, with pop-guns and swords and daggers. I shall dig a cavern underground where the young ones can hide."

"Will there be anything to eat?" asked Hare.

"The Weasels will do the eating if we don't stop their advance," replied Moldy Warp coolly.

"I thought there would be sandwiches provided, " said Hare sorrowfully. "I can't fight on an empty stomach."

Just then a crow came cawing to the garden.

"They are coming afar off, Moldy Warp. They are sweeping everything before them. They will be here before the sun gets over the sky."

"Every animal to his post," commanded Mole. "Get ready to meet those invaders and turn them back."

Away they all rushed to find weapons and to carry out Mole's secret plan. The mice cut sharp thorns from the hawthorns and made barricades across the warpath. The rabbits made pop-guns of elder, and collected stones for bullets.

Then, under Hedgehog's directions, they dragged branches of prickly furze to the Roman road. The squirrels bent the slender hazel saplings into bows and filled their little fur pockets with arrows. The hedgehogs sharpened their quills and stood ready. Wise Owl flew over the woods, keeping watch and ward. Robin the Postman had a bow and a sheath of feathered arrows. The Speckledy Hen and the Red Cock came armed with their sharp beaks and spurs.

The Water-rat sat in his boat with a long spear made from water-reeds.

Under the earth, deep in the soil, worked Moldy Warp. He dug with his strong little feet and hands, and hollowed out a cave next to his own stronghold for all the baby rabbits and mice and hedgehogs.

"Come inside," he called, when Fuzzypeg strolled up to see the mole-hills he had thrown in the field.

"Come inside and look how nice it is for the youngsters."

Fuzzypeg stepped carefully down the stairway into the ground and entered the large room.

There were grass hammocks hanging from the roots of the tree, and wool-lined cots and cradles Grey Rabbit had made. On the floor were toys for the babies. Round the walls were glow-worms, shining with soft green lights.

"You shall take charge of the young ones, Fuzzypeg," said Moldy Warp kindly. Fuzzypeg shook his head indignantly.

"No, thank you! I'm going to fight."

"You can't fight, little Fuzzypeg! Your prickles are not strong enough."

"Oh no," protested Fuzzypeg. "I've got the ammunition. I've got the old eggs hidden away for the foe. The eggs are older than me, and they will go off with such a bang! Hare's making himself a gas-mask!"

"All right, stout fellow," laughed Moldy Warp. "I'll ask your mother to take care of the babies."

Inside Grey Rabbit's house all was bustle and stir. Hare ran upstairs and downstairs calling: "Grey Rabbit! Where's my catapult? Grey Rabbit! Where's my haversack? Grey Rabbit! Where's my helmet? Where's my red coat? Where's my umbrella? Where's my pistol? Make some sandwiches, Grey Rabbit."

Squirrel was knitting so fast she used eight needles at once. Sheep's wool was twined round the legs of chairs and twisted about the table, but Squirrel never stopped for a mere ravel. She knotted wool and knitted away.

Little socks and mittens and helmets fell to the floor as she made them, and she broke off the wool and started another garment.

Little Grey Rabbit sewed a Red Cross on her blue apron. She tore up a sheet for bandages, and she packed a pin-cushion with thorns for pins. She fetched her ointments and her cures for all hurts, and she brewed some herb tea ready for the wounded. She made some sticking-plaster with the sweet gum of the larch-trees.

Hare strutted up and down with his catapult. On his head he wore a saucepan, and covering his chest was a dish-cover. He carried his gas-mask on his back, and round his waist was a belt which held an ancient toy pistol.

"Why do you want a butterfly net?" asked Grey Rabbit.

"That's a gas-mask," said Hare proudly. "I shall wear it when Fuzzypeg throws the old-laid eggs."

"Too-whit! Too-whoo!" called Wise Owl in a long-drawn cry. "Too-whoo-oo-oo-oo! Get to your places. They are coming near."

An army of Weasels was marching along the old grass covered Roman road. Their teeth shone white, their noses were raised, their little fierce eyes looked here and there, as their long thin bodies moved swiftly over the ground.

Moldy Warp was working furiously at a trench which cut the old road. Deeper and deeper he went, and a band of rabbits with wheelbarrows were piling the soil high. Old Hedgehog stood with his prickles like a gorse bush. He rolled himself into a ball and hid in the shadows. Overhead flew Wise Owl, with never a sound of his soft wings.

"What's all this about?" asked Hare, marching up with his weapons jingling like a cart-horse's brasses.

"Silence!" hissed Mole, throwing a shower of earth upon him.

"What are you making?" whispered Hare, leaning over the trench to look at Mole.

"An ambush," muttered Moldy Warp.

"A hambush!" echoed Hare, and he walked off to find Grey Rabbit and Squirrel.

"Mole's making an egg-bush," said he. "No, a hambush. Ham and eggs for the Weasels," he explained.

At last the deep trench was finished, and the animals threw their sharp thorns and furze bushes over the bottom of the long pit.

Across the top they spread a layer of twigs, so delicately placed that they would snap with the lightest touch. Squirrels dropped grasses over the gap, and Robin the Postman came with a mail-bag full of leaf letters to sprinkle.

Mole mopped his forehead.

"Now hide yourselves with your pop-guns and don't move a whisker," he told the rabbits.

"Squirrels, all of you climb the trees and wait with your bows and arrows."

So the Squirrels climbed the trees and the little rabbits hid in the bushes, with their pop-guns pointing towards the pit in the lane.

Fuzzypeg and his cousins were crouched behind some dock-leaves, and in the nettle-bed beside them were the old-laid eggs.

"Throw your bombs in the trench when the Weasels fall into it," said Moldy Warp.

Fuzzypeg and his cousins, Tim and Bill Hedgehog seized the bad eggs and jigged with excitement.

"Can we really throw at the Weasels?" asked Tim and Bill.

"Yes, and mind you don't miss!"

Hare came up dressed in his Home Guard uniform. His haversack was filled with sandwiches.

"Have a bite?" he asked, and he held out a sandwich to the small hedgehogs.

"Oh, thank you, Hare. Thank you, sir," they cried. "You do look brave, Hare."

Squirrel came running up with a bundle of garments under her arm. She tossed them to the waiting rabbits, and they muffled their feet in gloves and mittens. Squirrel sat down by the ambush and went on with her knitting.

"Be ready with your bombs, and throw them at the enemy."

Tramp! Tramp! went the feet of the Weasels down the green lane towards Grey Rabbit's house. Their long bodies moved in snaky columns as they followed their leader.

Suddenly Wise Owl dropped like a stone and carried off the big Weasel at the front of the army.

The rest squealed in surprise. Those at the back marched on and the foremost were pushed on the thin layer of twigs over the pit. Down they went, one on top of another, into the ambush.

"Fire! Fire!" shouted Moldy Warp and bang went his old blunderbuss among them!

Then Fuzzypeg and Tim and Bill Hedgehog threw the old-laid eggs. Every egg hit a weasel and knocked over a dozen others. Pouf! What a smell there was!

Hare put on his gas-mask and fired his sandwiches from his catapult by mistake. It wasn't till his haversack was empty that he discovered his mistake.

The Weasels struggled and fought and rolled about in the pit.

"A trap!" they cried, and they climbed on each other's backs and scrambled out.

But arrow after arrow dropped among them, and Old Hedgehog rolled after them, and Water-rat threw his long spear, and the Speckledy Hen and the Cock pecked at them. Then Wise Owl swooped down again, and that was the end.

The Weasels gave loud cries of terror and away they went, over the fields, across the woods many a mile to their own wild country.

On the battle-field Grey Rabbit the
Red Cross nurse attended to the wounded.

Mrs Hedgehog carried bowls of hot pea-
soup to the tired little animals, and Old
Hedgehog came hurrying up with a can of
warm milk.

Down the lane came Moldy Warp and
Fuzzypeg, and behind them the crowd of
little rabbits and hedgehogs and mice who
had been in Moldy Warp's cavern.

"Hurrah for Moldy Warp the leader!"
cried the little army, and they waved their
caps and mufflers and scarves.

"Hurrah for little Fuzzypeg the bomber!
Hurrah for Grey Rabbit the Red Cross
nurse, and Squirrel the knitter and Hare
the Home Guard!"